Lie Detector

Truth Detector   *   Monitor Thirteen

by   Peter Yates

Lie Detector

by   Peter Yates

©COPYRIGHT 2006, 2009 Peter Yates

First Published 2009 by Random Cactus
ISBN: 978-0-9559924-0-7

Rights of Performance are controlled by:

Random Cactus
New Place,
Romeland Hill,
St. Albans,
Herts.
AL3 4ET
Phone: 01727 838540
Fax: 01727 843540
Email: random_cactus@yahoo.co.uk
Web: www.randomcactus.co.uk

from whom a license for performance should be obtained.

It is an infringement of the Copyright to give any performance or public reading of the play before the license has been issued.

Lie Detector

Was originally performed at Theatre 503, London, April 2006, with the following cast:

James Flynn as **Thorpe**
Jennifer Taylor as **Beaulieu**

Directed by Marie Bobin
Produced by Practicum Theatre

Lie Detector, Truth Detector & Monitor Thirteen

were performed at Roman Eagle Lodge at the Edinburgh Fringe, August 2007, with the following cast:

James Flynn   Thorpe, Doctor, Hunt
Jennifer Taylor   Beaulieu, Woman
Samuel Collings   Official, Leach
Chris Bhantoa   Warden, Agent

Lighting & Sound by Laura Gill
Directed by Marie Bobin

Produced by Peter Yates & Marie Bobin for Random Cactus

A version of **Lie Detector** with

Reuben Anderson as **Thorpe**
Mariele Runacre Temple as **Beaulieu**

was recorded for *the* **wireless theatre company**
and is available to download from:

www.wirelesstheatrecompany.co.uk

Lie Detector

Characters:

Thorpe

Beaulieu

An Interrogation Room. Now.

A sparsely lit room. A table. Swivel chair on each side. On the table a walkie-talkie, a bottle of water, a packet of cigarettes and lighter.

Thorpe**, in suit with open-neck shirt, sits one side.* ***Beaulieu, *more casual, sits on the other. She has a note-pad.*

THORPE: [*Coughs*]

BEAULIEU: OK, Mr. Thorpe?

THORPE: Yes.

BEAUL: Water?

THORPE: No.

BEAUL: We start with control questions. Your name is Paul Thorpe?

THORPE: No.

BEAUL: Your name is Paul Jameson Thorpe?

THORPE: Yes.

BEAUL: Your address is 14, The Parkway, Barnes…?

THORPE: Yes.

BEAUL: You are a systems analyst?

THORPE: Yes.

BEAUL: You are married?

THORPE: Yes.

BEAUL: You have three children?

THORPE: Yes.

BEAUL: You were born in Hampton, England.

THORPE: That's what it says on my passport.

BEAUL: Is that an affirmative answer, Mr. Thorpe?

THORPE: Take it as you wish.

BEAUL: I need a positive or negative response. These are control questions...

THORPE: Yes...?

BEAUL: Repeat. You were born in Hampton, England?

THORPE: Yes.

BEAUL: Your favourite drink is tea?

THORPE: Yes.

BEAUL: You were involved in the Amen Corner Drugs Smuggling Operation.

THORPE: Yes.

*An intermittent buzzer sounds; a red flashing light reflects on **Thorpe's** face.*

BEAUL: According to this, Mr. Thorpe, that is a lie.

THORPE: Well, that's what you want me to say, isn't it? That's why I'm here?

BEAUL: I want the truth, Mr. Thorpe. Only the truth. That was a lie.

THORPE: Maybe all the control answers were lies.

BEAUL: What…?

THORPE: That's how these things work, isn't it? You ask a series of control questions. Get a level. Then when the reading goes above the control level – bingo. It's a lie. But if that control level has been based on lies…

*Pause. **Beaulieu** writes something on her pad – playing for time.*

THORPE: Can I go now? Apparently I didn't do it. I'm not involved in Amen Corner. According to you. According to your… apparatus. Am I free to go?

BEAUL: [*regaining composure*] According to regulations, Mr. Thorpe, ten minutes is the maximum continuous stint in a full respondent session with a minimum two minute break before continuing. Questioning suspended. Do you require the rest room, Mr. Thorpe?

THORPE: Yes.

Buzzer sounds, red flashing light.

BEAUL: [*irritated, flustered; into w/t*] Switch off. It's a break. Sorry. Do you require the rest room?

THORPE: [*highly amused*] No. I was lying.

BEAUL: Cigarette? Water?

THORPE: [*taking off jacket*] I'm fine. Fine and dandy.

*LX change: **Thorpe** in shadow, **Beaulieu** in spot, looking away from **Thorpe**, staring into distance.*

BEAUL: Cigarette. Water. Bread. Milk. Olives. Nibbles. Cigarettes. Benson and Hedges. Lambert and Butler. Senior Service. Passing Clouds. Capstan. Woodbines. Players Number Six. My granddad smoked them all. And he kept all the packets. Stacked up on the dresser. In his little house in Hay-on-Wye. I use to visit him in the holidays. And I use to count them, the packets. And stack them neatly. On the dresser. And the Davenport. And the ancient radiogram. I used to recite the names. And build castles out of them. In the holidays. Summer. Sun. Carefree. Hot. Water. Cigarettes. Water....

THORPE: How long's the break?

LX snaps back.

BEAUL: Further control questions, Mr. Thorpe.

THORPE: The anticipation is tangible.

BEAUL: Are you ready, Mr. Thorpe?

THORPE: Is that a control question?

BEAUL: Water?

Thorpe *Indicates no.*

BEAUL: [*into w/t*] Resume. Your name is Paul Thorpe?

THORPE: No.

BEAUL: Your name is Paul Jameson Thorpe?

THORPE: No.

BEAUL: Your name is Doctor Paul Jameson Thorpe?

THORPE: Yes.

BEAUL: Your address is 14, The Parkway, Barnes…?

THORPE: No.

Beat.

BEAUL: You are a systems analyst?

THORPE: No.

BEAUL: You are married?

THORPE: No.

BEAUL: You have three children?

THORPE: No.

BEAUL: You were born in Hampton, England.

THORPE: It's not what it says on my passport.

BEAUL: Is that a negative answer, Mr. Thorpe?

THORPE: Take it as you wish.

BEAUL: I need a positive or negative response. These are control questions…

THORPE: Yes…?

BEAUL: Repeat. You were born in Hampton, England?

THORPE: No.

BEAUL: Your favourite drink is tea?

THORPE: No.

BEAUL: Your favourite drink is… wine?

THORPE: Yes.

BEAUL: Your favourite wine is…

THORPE: Italian.

BEAUL: Your favourite Italian wine is…

THORPE: Chianti. It has a light, fruity palette with a soft bouquet and is a particularly suitable accompaniment to…

BEAUL: Chicken.

THORPE: …tomato dishes and braised rabbit.

BEAUL: [*distracted*] Chicken pasta dishes like... I like it with... it goes with... You were involved in the so-called Amen Corner drugs smuggling ring that has been positively connected to the *Jihad Now!* Terror Organisation.

THORPE: No. Never. Not me.

Buzzer sounds, red flashing light.

BEAUL: That is a lie, Mr. Thorpe. According to this.

THORPE: That's intriguing, don't you think. If I say yes, it's a lie. If I say no, it's a lie. Could I ask if you have full confidence in your er... equipment, Ms Beaulieu?

BEAUL: I am conducting this examination, Mr. Thorpe. I...

THORPE: [*amused*] Oh, please! Don't say "I ask the questions".

BEAUL: I am conducting this examination. [*pause*] Why did you call me Beaulieu?

THORPE: It's your name. Isn't it?

BEAUL: No.

Buzzer sounds, red flashing light.

BEAUL: [*into w/t*] Break. Would you like the rest room, Mr. Thorpe?

THORPE: Is it off, now?

BEAUL: The rest room…?

THORPE: No.

BEAUL: Water? Cigarette? Exercise?

LX change as before.

BEAUL: Exercise. The gym. What is Gaynor's problem at the gym? I mean, she wears an ever more revealing suit every time she comes there. What is she trying to prove? That she is fitter than me? Has a better body than me? That she's more attractive to men than me? She wants to go on holiday again but if she's going to go on like that... Well, one thing's certain, she can't cook. Tonight – we'll settle that once and for all. When they come round. Chicken Cacciatore. My speciality. All the right herbs, fresh plum tomatoes, the special recipe. Never fails. Olives. Fine wine. [*pause*] Chianti. Goes well with it. I think. Doesn't it? Perhaps I should ask. He obviously knows about wine. In a break. Off the record. Nothing wrong with that, is there? We are trained to put the subject at their ease. Talk about other stuff.

THORPE: [*snaps fingers*] Is there something you want to ask me?

LX snaps back.

BEAUL: [*startled*] What – the Chianti...

THORPE: Sorry? Am I being accused of...

BEAUL: Sorry. Control questions complete. Tell me your relationship with Anwar Mahmoud.

THORPE: He runs the corner shop. General Stores. Off license. At the end of my street. I buy my wine from him. Chardonnay. Merlot. And Chianti.

BEAUL: Does Chianti go well with Chicken cacciatore?

THORPE: No.

Buzzer sounds, red flashing light.

BEAUL: That's a lie.

THORPE: Ask me again.

BEAUL: Does Chianti go well with Chicken cacciatore?

THORPE: Yes.

Buzzer sounds, red flashing light.

THORPE: Can you trust your equipment Ms. Beaulieu.

BEAUL: Don't call me that. I'm getting confused. I didn't mean to ask that question. Ignore it.

THORPE: Ignore the truth? Or the lies.

BEAUL: Anwar Mahmoud is a terrorist. You have been giving money to him to support his organisation. His organisation recruits and trains suicide bombers in this country. You're as guilty as hell, Mr. Thorpe and you know it.

THORPE: Is that the polygraph's view or your personal appraisal?

BEAUL: Are you denying it?

THORPE: I don't deny I gave a shop-keeper money. Are you treating everyone of his customers this way?

BEAUL: Your name was on his computer.

THORPE: Maybe I was next on his list.

BEAUL: What list?

THORPE: Of potential suicide bombers.

BEAUL: You don't strike me as the type.

THORPE: Because I drink Chianti? Or do you mean I'm not young, fanatical, brown-skinned and Moslem.

BEAUL: Though you do visit Hadley Vale Mosque on a regular basis.

THORPE: I'm a building contractor. They need an extension.

BEAUL: You've been to Pakistan on several occasions.

THORPE: I like cricket.

BEAUL: You've given money to an irrigation project in Afghanistan.

THORPE: I'm a philanthropist.

BEAUL: Did you support the war in Iraq?

THORPE: No.

BEAUL: What is your opinion on Israel's protective barrier?

THORPE: It's there.

BEAUL: Do you support it.

THORPE: No. [*pause*] It's a self-supporting structure.

BEAUL: [*irritated*] Do you believe that Iran should be free to develop its own nuclear programme?

THORPE: Yes.

BEAUL: Do you support President Bush's foreign policy.

THORPE: No.

BEAUL: Are you or have you ever been a practising homosexual?

THORPE: [*pause*] What kind of question is that?

BEAUL: Are you or have you ever been a practising homosexual?

THORPE: No.

Buzzer sounds, red flashing light.

THORPE: Yes.

BEAUL: I'll ask again. Are you or have you ever been a practising homosexual?

THORPE: Yes – and no.

BEAUL: That's two answers.

THORPE: It was two questions.

BEAUL: You think you're pretty smart, don't you, Mr. Thorpe?

THORPE: Yes.

Buzzer sounds, red flashing light.

THORPE: What do you make of that, then, Ms Beaulieu?

BEAUL: I…er… I don't know.

THORPE: Have you got low self-esteem, Ms Beaulieu?

BEAUL: No!

Buzzer sounds, red flashing light.

BEAUL: OK. Yes. Maybe. Yes. OK? What the fuck has it got to do with you?

THORPE: I might well ask you the same question, Ms Beaulieu. Of all these questions. What the fuck have they got to do with you? I'm an ordinary citizen who, during the course of going about my ordinary, everyday business, has made some coincidental contacts with someone who may be a terrorist or may just be another ordinary citizen who also has some coincidental contacts but suddenly I'm bankrolling suicide bombers. And the proof of this? A piece of ultra-sophisticated polygraph equipment which has shown itself – and its operator - to be totally fallible. Totally fallible. Do you believe the machine, Ms. Beaulieu? Or are you going with your gut feeling? Are going to release me? Or are you going to look the other way?

BEAUL: I don't have gut feelings, Mr. Thorpe. I am not allowed to have gut feelings. This is a scientific analysis. It circumvents the presence of human fallibility. If I do my job properly then...

THORPE: The citizens of this country can be locked up without the need for instinct, subjectivity, reality, or truth. Justice isn't necessary. Plausibility is all. Lock me up, Ms. Beaulieu. Throw away the key. Put me in an orange jump suit. The machine says I lied. The machine never lies. The machine says I'm guilty. But don't you lose any sleep, Ms. Beaulieu. It's not down to you. You merely interpret the data.

BEAUL: [*into w/t*] Break. Water, Mr. Thorpe?

LX change as before.

BEAUL: Water. Sea. Sand. Holidays. I need a holiday. That's what I need. A holiday. This is a very demoralising job. I'm always inside. Never out in the air. Always analysing. Asking questions. Assessing answers. Making judgements. Reviewing the evidence. On the balance of probabilities. On balance this. On balance that. I need some sand. I need some sea. I need Florida. I need freedom. In the land of the free. This guy... he's not... he's probably not... on the balance of probabilities...

LX change.

THORPE: [*takes out tie from his pocket and starts to put it on*] I'm still here. What's the verdict? Am I guilty? As charged. Am I someone who pays people to blow themselves up in tube stations for the greater glory of Islam and loves to read it in the newspapers the next day? On the balance of probabilities am I a fanatic? Ms Beaulieu?

BEAUL: Why have they allowed you to keep your tie? [*picks up w/t*] This session is now complete. Recommendation: on the data received, the subject should proceed to stage two.

THORPE: Stage two?

BEAUL: Forceful inducement.

THORPE: Forceful inducement?

BEAUL: It means what it says.

THORPE: Sensory depravation. Isolation. Torture. But, no doubt, not on this soil. Do you think, on balance, I deserve that?

BEAUL: I merely operate the system, Mr. Thorpe.

THORPE: Ah. You mean you just carry out orders.

BEAUL: I interpret the data. This is a lie detector. You are a liar.

THORPE: Harsh.

BEAUL: Just because you drink Chianti, Mr. Thorpe, does not preclude you from being a liar.

THORPE: Did you know that the distinctive squat bottle in a basket that identifies Chianti is called a "fiasco"? [*indicates w/t*] May I?

BEAUL: What...?

THORPE: [*picks up w/t, standing*] Chief Operative Dexter. I cannot recommend Junior Operative Beaulieu for promotion at this time. Too personally involved. Analysis terminated.

Thorpe *puts on jacket.*

THORPE: You seem a little shocked. Water? Cigarette? Do you need the rest room? [*pause*] I have an appointment. If you'll excuse me. [*pause*] Take a holiday. I think you need it.

***Thorpe** exits.*

BEAUL: I don't. Honestly. I don't need a holiday.

Buzzer sounds, red flashing light.

*Fade to **Blackout.***

Truth Detector

Truth Detector

by Peter Yates

©COPYRIGHT 2007, 2009 Peter Yates

First Published 2009 by Random Cactus
ISBN: 978-0-9559924-0-7

Rights of Performance are controlled by:

Random Cactus
New Place,
Romeland Hill,
St. Albans,
Herts.
AL3 4ET
Phone: 01727 838540
Fax: 01727 843540
Email: random_cactus@yahoo.co.uk
Web: www.randomcactus.co.uk

from whom a license for performance should be obtained.

It is an infringement of the Copyright to give any performance or public reading of the play before the license has been issued.

Characters:

Woman

Warden

Official

Doctor

Agent

Great Britain. Today.

1.

>*Woman DSC with remote car key which she uses [FX] and then walks towards exit. Warden appears.*

WARDEN: Excuse me, madam. Are you looking for the Passport Office?

WOMAN: Yes, I am actually. But I know where it is. It's round the corner.

WARDEN: I'm afraid, though, madam, you can't park here.

WOMAN: I beg your pardon?

WARDEN: I said, madam, you cannot park here.

WOMAN: Why not? There are no parking restrictions in force here. Absolutely none. None at all.

WARDEN: I beg to differ, madam. I am the sole arbiter of parking restrictions in this area. I am divested with the authority to allow or not to allow parking here, on any given day at any given time.

WOMAN: But I work near here. I always park here.

WARDEN: Not today, madam.

WOMAN: That's outrageous. Why not today?

WARDEN: I'm afraid I am not at liberty to divulge that information, madam.

WOMAN: Why on earth not? It's only parking, after all.

WARDEN: National Security.

WOMAN: Oh, don't make me laugh. National Security? Poppycock!

WARDEN: [writing] Poppycock. I must warn you, madam, it is an offence under the National Security Act of 2009 to belittle or satirize any aspect of National Security.

WOMAN: This is 2008, sunshine. 2009 is NEXT YEAR. Doh!

WARDEN: The legislation has been post-dated.

WOMAN: What?

WARDEN: Post-dated. Like a cheque. The legislation is destined for 2009. But when it comes into force it will be retrospective. So by calling a matter of National Security "poppycock" you are breaking the law.

WOMAN: Piffle!

WARDEN: [*writing*] P-i-f ... is that one f or two f's?

WOMAN: Complete fucking piffle. That's three f's.

WARDEN: It is, madam, an offence to use profane language in the street.

WOMAN: Piffle isn't profane.

WARDEN: No, but "fucking" is.

WOMAN: It is, sir, an offence to use profane language in the street.

WARDEN: [*pause*] Very amusing, madam. Very clever. I should warn you, though, not to be too clever when dealing with the representatives of law and order in this nation.

WOMAN: Law and order, is it? You're just a Traffic Warden. You deal with yellow lines and resident permits and restrictions on loading between the hours of thirteen minutes past three and seven minutes past four in the early hours of Saturday morning. You deal with parking! That's it. Give a man a uniform and he thinks he's running the country.

WARDEN: I am very proud to wear this uniform, madam. It is a constant reminder that this nation was once great. And could be great again.

WOMAN: Oh come on…

WARDEN: Besides, another piece of legislation, of which you may not be aware, states that in times of national emergency then all personnel in uniform are invested with full military powers.

WOMAN: Ah! I see. So in my evening job as Miss Whiplash, which requires me to wear knee-high boots, a leather tunic and peaked cap – very definitely a uniform, wouldn't you say – I have licence to go round blowing away suspected terrorists with my plastic Kalashnikov. But, frankly, I'm not sure I want to spend much more of my life in idle chit-chat about the niceties of the law. So if you've said your piece I'll be on my way.

WARDEN: Wearing my public servant's hat, madam, I was merely trying to be helpful in explaining the law. But I see there is not much point in pursuing it. You are not allowed to park here. Please move your car.

WOMAN: It's not my car.

WARDEN: Ah. But you were driving it.

WOMAN: No I wasn't.

WARDEN: Yes you were.

WOMAN: No. I wasn't. Do you have evidence? Of me driving it?

WARDEN: Can you prove that you weren't? Driving it?

WOMAN: What? Don't be silly. I don't have to. Do I?

WARDEN: Madam, according to an important though barely noticed clause in the Government's Terrorism Bill 2006 – and I'm quoting here: if a suspect is within the vicinity – and there is a defined area for the purposes of the law – of a vehicle that contains an explosive device, then that is counted as ample evidence of implication of planting said device and leaves the suspect liable to arrest on suspicion of planting the device unless the suspect can prove non-ownership.

WOMAN: But there is no explosive device in this cream and black, six-ninety-eight cc, eco-friendly, park-in-a-shoe-box Smart Car.

WARDEN: How do you know? You said it wasn't your car.

WOMAN: It's a Smart Car! I wouldn't be seen dead in a Smart Car.

WARDEN: Prophetic words, perhaps, madam.

WOMAN: Well search the damn thing if you think there is.

WARDEN: Yes, and while I'm searching it what will you – the prime suspect for planting the device – do? Stand and watch? Or perhaps run away. I wasn't born yesterday, madam.

WOMAN: Well, as I didn't plant it I'll stand and watch.

WARDEN: Plant what, madam? Is it a small incendiary device? A gravity explosive? A pipe bomb? A shaped charge? A grenade? A dirty bomb? A sticky bomb? Napalm, neutron or even a nuclear bomb? We just don't know, do we? And as you, the prime suspect, is unlikely to tell us, or even admit to there actually being one in the car, we have to call the bomb squad.

WOMAN: Look, I'm sorry, but now this really is getting utterly ridiculous.

WARDEN: So madam is prepared to be blown to smithereens rather than suffer a little inconvenience while the security services go about their highly risky and heroic employment?

WOMAN: You're starting to talk in riddles. I'm going.

Loudspeaker: "Do not leave the area! Woman in red, do not leave the area!"

WOMAN: What...?

WARDEN: Sorry, madam. I had to activate the area alarm.

WOMAN: Activate...? What...? How...?

WARDEN: Actually it's quite clever. It will amuse you while you wait. [*she starts to move. Shouting*] Because you must seriously refrain from moving now! [*pause*] I can do it all from this little remote key-pad here.

WOMAN: Well, what will they think of next? How can it tell that I'm wearing red? Or that I'm a woman?

WARDEN: I just have to key in the right code. Woman in red. Youth in hoodie. Moslem with rucksack. Unidentified in Berka. Clever, eh?

WOMAN: And you have to know all the codes.

WARDEN: Absolutely. All part of our training.

WOMAN: So what happens now?

WARDEN: We wait. For the Bomb Squad to arrive.

WOMAN: The Bomb Squad? That's a bit over the top, isn't it?

WARDEN: Yes. But this is Britain. In the 21st century.

> The **Bomb Squad** sequence.
>
> **LX** change, **music**, slow-motion, exaggerated movements.
>
> **Official** and **Doctor** appear wearing long, black coats, carrying folding chairs like riot-shields, whistles in mouths. They pull **Warden** behind shields and crouch on floor for protection. **Woman** is left **DSC** trying to use her remote car key. **Warden** holds shields in place as **Official** and **Doctor** break cover to retrieve **Woman** and pull her behind shields. Once there, she stands up again, remonstrating; **Official** and **Doctor** put hands on her head to ease her down again.
>
> **Music** cuts, **LX** change, normal motion: **Official** and **Doctor** stand, let-off party poppers straight up in the air, streamers fall and land on **Woman's** head as **Warden**, **Official** and **Doctor** disappear.
>
> **Woman** is left pulling streamers from her hair as **LX** returns to normal state.

2.

VOICE-OVER: Number Fifty-three million, four hundred and twenty-seven thousand, two hundred and forty-nine.

> **LX** *up on a very high desk.* **Official**, *wielding an over-sized pencil, peers over the top at* **Woman** *who is still pulling streamers from her hair.*

OFFICIAL: Good Morning, madam. My name is Gerald Lowe. I am Acting Assistant Deputy Passport Registrar, Second Grade pending full Home Office confirmation. How are you today? Did you come by Tube? Bus? Car? Did you have any trouble parking?

WOMAN: Don't go there. I need a new Passport.

OFFICIAL: Fill in this form. Send it off.

WOMAN: Er... I've done that. And I was told I had to come here and apply personally.

OFFICIAL: That's right. Everyone has to do that. It's the law.

WOMAN: So... why don't you say that straight away? On the form?

OFFICIAL: The Complaints Department is down the corridor, first door on the right.

WOMAN: If I go down there I'll lose my place in the queue.

OFFICIAL: Quite.

WOMAN: And I've been waiting two and a half days.

OFFICIAL: Really? Have we got it down to that? Excellent. It was four days only last week. Someone's in for a bonus.

WOMAN: Look. I've had to miss work. I called in sick. Is this going to take long?

OFFICIAL: It depends entirely on your application madam. You are a British citizen?

WOMAN: Yes.

OFFICIAL: And you were born in...

WOMAN: London.

OFFICIAL: At...

WOMAN: St. Mary's, Paddington.

OFFICIAL: St. Mary's Hospital.

WOMAN: Yes. That's right.

OFFICIAL: Paddington.

WOMAN: Yes.

OFFICIAL: Are you absolutely certain about that?

WOMAN: What?

OFFICIAL: Are you...

WOMAN: Yes! Of course I'm certain.

OFFICIAL: Have you any evidence?

WOMAN: You've got my birth certificate there. The original, not a copy.

OFFICIAL: [*reading*] Ms. Tennant. Charlotte Agnes. Charlotte. Can I call you that?

WOMAN: If you must.

OFFICIAL: Such a pretty name. Charlotte. Any one can forge a birth certificate, Charlotte.

WOMAN: Can they?

OFFICIAL: Oh, yes. And some of them aren't too clever at it. I'm running at about four David Beckham's a day, at the moment. I get Gordon Brown – though less popular these days, I grant you. Will Windsor. Shilpa Shetty. Harold Pinter.

WOMAN: Really?

OFFICIAL: Well Harold Pinter turned out to be genuine, though. When I said: "Can you prove it?" there was a long pause. Then he said: "Give me my passport you little shit or I'll send the boys round". Menacing.

WOMAN: Yes, well this is all very interesting but how do I prove I was born where I was if you won't accept the birth certificate?

OFFICIAL: Parents? They were there, weren't they?

WOMAN: Dad wasn't and Mum's dead.

OFFICIAL: Grand parents?

WOMAN: All dead.

OFFICIAL: Ah. I see. Tricky. Well what we usually suggest is doctors, nurses, midwives.

WOMAN: I'm sorry?

OFFICIAL: See if you can track down any of the staff at the hospital when you were born.

WOMAN: It's twenty-seven years ago. Who's going to remember a single baby's birth all that long ago?

OFFICIAL: Well, we usually recommend you bung 'em a monkey. Helps the memory. It's amazing what they can recall with that little incentive.

WOMAN: Bung 'em a monkey?

OFFICIAL: 500 quid, yes. We have a full database – I can print you off the complete list of staff at St Mary's in er... 1981? With last known contact numbers. Cost you a tenner, that's all.

WOMAN: And what bit of the monkey do you get, then?

OFFICIAL: Oh, Miss Tennant! Charlotte, please! I am a Civil Servant. I do not take back-handers. It's against my religion. Which is the perfect link. What's yours?

WOMAN: A large Gin and Tonic.

OFFICIAL: Religion, Charlotte.

WOMAN: Oh, sorry. Not sure I see the relevance, though.

OFFICIAL: Well... if you'd like to send in the next...

WOMAN: OK. C of E.

OFFICIAL: C. of E?

WOMAN: Church of England.

OFFICIAL: From birth?

WOMAN: Yes... assuming I was actually born... seeing as the authenticity of my birth certificate is being called into question.

OFFICIAL: Now, now, Charlotte. We wouldn't want a hint of sarcasm to delay your chances of getting a passport now, would we?

WOMAN: Sorry. Church of England. From Birth.

OFFICIAL: Are you in regular attendance at your local Mosque?

WOMAN: Mosque? You mean church, don't you?

OFFICIAL: Oh, silly me. Sorry. Church, of course.

WOMAN: Not really, no.

OFFICIAL: But... have you ever been to a Mosque?

WOMAN: What is this?

OFFICIAL: Have you...

WOMAN: No I haven't. And I don't see what difference it makes...

OFFICIAL: Could you identify the woman in this picture?

WOMAN: Where did you get...? Well, yes, it looks like me.

OFFICIAL: Outside Regent's Park Mosque.

WOMAN: Which I walk past every day on my way to work. Who took...?

OFFICIAL: Never popped inside to take a peek?

WOMAN: Never. You can't just take random photos...

OFFICIAL: But you can see how this might be misinterpreted...

WOMAN: But anyone can forge a photograph, can't they, Mr. Lowe?

OFFICIAL: Possibly. So you have never had any contact at all with any Moslems in your whole life? Ever?

WOMAN: Well, I don't know. Maybe. I'm not in the habit of asking everyone I meet what religion they are. Do you?

OFFICIAL: I'm not applying for a passport. But I think in the near future that's exactly what the government will want us to do. Ascertain the religion of everyone we meet.

WOMAN: Wouldn't it be easier to give everyone a badge for swift determination of the threat their religion might pose.

OFFICIAL: Yes. That's certainly an interesting idea. I'll pass it on, up. Suggestions?

WOMAN: Christians a cross, I suppose.

OFFICIAL: Broad brush, Charlotte. You'd need to narrow it down into sects and schisms.

WOMAN: OK. C. of E. – Gay Bishop with "No" stamped over?

OFFICIAL: I like that, yes. Methodists?

WOMAN: Pint of lager crossed out?

OFFICIAL: Good. RC?

WOMAN: Condom with an X through it?

OFFICIAL: Very good. Moslems?

OFFICIAL/WOMAN: An exploding rucksack!

OFFICIAL: Excellent. Which brings us nicely on to Ethnicity. Ethnic origin?

WOMAN: I don't have to answer that. Do I?

OFFICIAL: I'm afraid you do.

WOMAN: Female White Caucasian. Will that do?

OFFICIAL: Yes. Have you always been white?

Woman looks blank.

OFFICIAL: Ms. Tennant? Charlotte?

WOMAN: What are you talking about?

OFFICIAL: Well you just have to look at Michael Jackson. He was black. Once. It's amazing what lengths these terrorists will go to in order to infiltrate society.

WOMAN: I'm not a terrorist. And you're not telling me Michael Jackson is, are you?

OFFICIAL: Not necessarily. And yes, Charlotte, I'm sure you're not. But if you were, you would say that, wouldn't you?

WOMAN: I'm not a liar, Mr. Lowe.

OFFICIAL: Have you ever called in sick at work when you weren't ill?

WOMAN: Well… look… if I was black and now I'm white, there'd be no way of proving I was black once, and conversely, if I wasn't black, but white, and I'm still white, how am I meant to prove that I was never black but always white?

OFFICIAL: Yes, yes. I see where you're coming from. Difficult. Birth Certificate could be forged. Photos, as you rightly point out, can be air-brushed. Hospital workers could be bribed. Relations could all have been massacred, ha ha! So you can't really. Prove it.

WOMAN: It's crazy.

OFFICIAL: Don't worry. Everyone else is in the same boat.

WOMAN: No wonder it takes so long to process these passports.

OFFICIAL: Yes. Especially as most are rejected the first few times.

WOMAN: What?

OFFICIAL: It's true. They are really cracking down. But look, Charlotte. You seem genuine enough to me. Let me give you a little piece of advice.

WOMAN: What's it going to cost me?

OFFICIAL: Oh, Charlotte! Such cynicism in one so young. Nothing at all. Though, of course, if you felt the advice was helpful you might possibly want to show your appreciation by supporting a little good cause that is near to my heart.

WOMAN: Which is...?

OFFICIAL: [*holds up leaflet*] Sponsor a Free Range Turkey.

WOMAN: A trifle esoteric, Mr. Lowe. What's the advice?

OFFICIAL: Get yourself an ID card.

WOMAN: But ID cards are not compulsory. The Government has explicitly said that they have been introduced on an entirely voluntary basis.

OFFICIAL: Yes. That's what they say. But I can give you an absolute assurance, Charlotte, that if you have an ID card, getting a passport will take two and a half minutes, not two and a half days.

WOMAN: Right...

OFFICIAL: Moreover, it's three strikes and you're out

WOMAN: What?

OFFICIAL: If your passport is refused thee times you can't apply again for five years...

WOMAN: No...

OFFICIAL: ...and your name goes on the Illegal Immigrants' Register.

WOMAN: You're having a laugh.

OFFICIAL: You really don't want me to refuse this application, Charlotte, do you? I could mark it "Pending ID Card" in my day-glow orange hi-lighter.

WOMAN: You're not having a laugh. Are there no other exceptions?

OFFICIAL: Free Masons.

WOMAN: Er...

OFFICIAL: No, Charlotte. You're not a sad middle-aged male who likes silly rituals. You don't qualify. Suspected terrorists.

WOMAN: What?

OFFICIAL: Well, we give then a quick, hassle-free passport then find something wrong with it and lock 'em up.

WOMAN: Clever.

OFFICIAL: And Labour Party Donors. It's called cash for holidays. Again, I don't think you qualify.

WOMAN: I don't have any choice, then.

OFFICIAL: Sign the Turkey sponsorship form or it's…

OFFICIAL/WOMAN: The Immigration Squad!

> The **Immigration Squad** Sequence.
>
> **LX** change, **music**, slow-motion, exaggerated movements.
>
> Clothes are thrown on stage, **Warden** is propelled after them and scrabbles around picking them up. As he tries to leave **SR Doctor** [long, black coat] appears and blocks his way. **Doctor** grabs him by the neck and forces him down, then flings him back towards **SL** where **Official** [long, black coat] has

*appeared. **Official** spins him around, sends him back to **SC** and **Official** and **Doctor** break into a crazy dance; they then pat **Warden** on the cheek and send him on his way. They follow him and all return with a folding chair that they place in a row in front of the high desk. **Doctor** exits as **Woman**, who has been watching, comes forward and **Official** hands her his over-sized pencil and the form which she signs. **Warden** holds up a handful of feathers which he blows in the air over **Woman**. **Official** and **Warden** exit as **Woman** goes to chairs, lies down, goes to sleep.*

3.

> ***Doctor**, in white coat, enters pulling a large toy fire-engine which contains his equipment, carrying a small folding table.*

DOCTOR: Good morning, Ms. Tennant.

> *He sits, squeezing onto the end of the row by Woman's head, sets up the table and arranges his equipment on it.*

WOMAN: You're wearing a white coat.

> *She sits up, drowsily coming round, pulling feathers from her hair.*

DOCTOR: I see you have been referred by Mr. Lowe.

WOMAN: Why are you wearing a white coat?

DOCTOR: In the passport office.

WOMAN: You're wearing a white coat. Why is that?

DOCTOR: I'm a doctor, madam.

WOMAN: A doctor? I thought this was the ID Card Directorate. I'm meant to be...

DOCTOR: It is, madam.

WOMAN: But...

DOCTOR: Yes, I know. It takes a lot of people by surprise. But technically ID card verification is based on biometrics and as that involves the various physiological attributes of the human body then it is your doctor who is the best qualified to perform the... er... operation, so to speak.

WOMAN: But you're not my doctor.

DOCTOR: Figure of speech. But if you are looking, or may in the future be looking, for a top private practitioner then here's my card. [*hands her a business card and looks at a form*] Now, a few routine questions. Reason for requiring ID card...

WOMAN: Identification?

DOCTOR: Sorry. They don't have a box for that. Driving Licence, no. Electoral roll – for voting purposes – no. Registering with the NHS or NPHS.

WOMAN: NPHS?

DOCTOR: National Private Health Service. Or, slightly more frivolously: passport.

WOMAN: Anything wrong with that?

DOCTOR: No. Nothing at all. But tacky short breaks to Magaluf, Zante or the Maldives are likely to be viewed less indulgently by the government as it tries to enhance its green credentials. Any idea about the size of your carbon footprint, Ms. Tennant?

WOMAN: Oh for fuck's sake. Can we just get on with this?

DOCTOR: Of course. Of course. Sorry. Just a little pet *cause célèbre* of mine.

WOMAN: You want me to sponsor a windmill in Tower Hamlets, is that it?

DOCTOR: No actually it's a new forest in Ardnamurchan [*leaflet*]. We can talk later if you're interested. Sorry.

WOMAN: Not at all. It's fascinating. Do carry on.

DOCTOR: Fingerprints.

WOMAN: [*offering hand*] Here.

DOCTOR: No, no. It's OK. No mucking about with those horribly messy ink pads. We have them already. Your prints.

WOMAN: You do? How?

DOCTOR: You had a cup of coffee in the waiting area? [*holding up cup*] Now those might have appeared to have been ordinary Styrofoam cups but they have been specially developed with a substance called ionic-krypto-carbonite to capture a good print of all digits that it comes into contact with.

WOMAN: Well, it could have been anyone's cup, anyone's prints.

DOCTOR: Did you get your cup from the dispenser?

WOMAN: No, it was empty.

DOCTOR: So you…

WOMAN: …had to ask the receptionist for one…

DOCTOR: …and the one she gave you was marked on the base [*shows*].

WOMAN: Right. So you've got my fingerprints. Is that it? Can I go now?

DOCTOR: Eyes. Colour?

WOMAN: Blue.

DOCTOR: Ah. But are they?

WOMAN: What?

DOCTOR: Everyone wants blue eyes. Likes to think they have blue eyes. But it's strange, isn't it? Statistically 13% of the population will have blue eyes. But 68% say they have for the purpose of passports and ID Cards. Yours are – greenish grey.

WOMAN: Well my boyfriend always tells me my eyes are purest blue.

DOCTOR: Boyfriends, eh? Can you trust them? Mine always tells me I have a lovely beside manner.

WOMAN: Ahem.

DOCTOR: Moving on we have your iris and retinal patterns on disc.

WOMAN: How…?

DOCTOR: The coffee machine. When you read the instructions it takes a photo of your eyes.

WOMAN: Really.

DOCTOR: Oh, yes. They'll be standard soon in every coffee, coke and other vending machines in the country.

WOMAN: I don't believe it.

DOCTOR: And condom machines. Buy a condom in the gents and it will measure the size of your...

WOMAN: I don't make a habit of frequenting the gents.

DOCTOR: [*standing*] Of course not. I'm sorry. Open wide.

WOMAN: What...?

DOCTOR: [*puts swab in her mouth*] DNA. Thank you.

WOMAN: Ugh!

DOCTOR: [*giving cup*] Water. Rinse. Spit.

Doctor stands over her and pulls out a hair.

WOMAN: Ow! What are you doing?

DOCTOR: Strand of hair. It is natural, your colour?

WOMAN: Yes, of course.

DOCTOR: Damn. Got a grey one.

WOMAN: I haven't got grey...

DOCTOR: We are currently recommending a special promotion of Garnier Hair Colourant if you're interested. [*shows packet*]

Doctor pulls out another hair.

WOMAN: Ow!

DOCTOR: Ah, that's better. Now let's see. Urine sample. [***Woman** starts to protest*] Don't worry, we got that when you visited the ladies in the waiting area. Blood. [*checking sheet*] You had a test on the

19th of April at St. Mary's Paddington – isn't that where you were born? See anyone you remembered there – no? So we don't need to concern ourselves with that.

WOMAN: You have some of my blood?

DOCTOR: Standard practice. All blood tests submit a sample to the national database. It's enshrined in law.

WOMAN: Don't tell me – a little known clause in the Terrorism Act 2006.

DOCTOR: You're well up on your Hansard, Ms. Tennant, if I may say so.

WOMAN: I do my best.

DOCTOR: Do you smoke?

WOMAN: No.

DOCTOR: Take recreational drugs?

WOMAN: No.

DOCTOR: Have you ever taken a recreational drug?

WOMAN: We all do things when we're young that we are not proud of later in life.

DOCTOR: Is that a yes?

WOMAN: It's a David Cameron-style "might have".

DOCTOR: I need a yes or a no.

WOMAN: Yes.

DOCTOR: Are you an alcoholic?

WOMAN: No.

DOCTOR: What is your favourite alcoholic drink?

WOMAN: What?

DOCTOR: Yes, it always breaks me up that one. What are they going to do – herd all the lager drinkers into one prison and the Champers lot into another?

WOMAN: Absinthe.

DOCTOR: Ah. You'll be in a prison on your own then. Any pets?

WOMAN: No.

DOCTOR: If you could choose, what holiday destination would you most like to go to?

WOMAN: Why on earth would they want to know that?

DOCTOR: Oh, they don't actually. I freelance for a Timeshare company and fill in the forms in parallel.

WOMAN: I'm not interested in Timeshares. I'm only interested in getting am ID card so I can get a passport so I can visit my boyfriend in Uzbekistan.

DOCTOR: I'll put down Uzbekistan then shall I? For your holiday destination. It's quite unusual. Get you extra points. Towards a free timeshare. Sorry.

WOMAN: Is that it?

DOCTOR: Almost! Teeth. All your own?

WOMAN: Yes.

DOCTOR: We have you're dental records of course.

WOMAN: Of course.

DOCTOR: [*reading*] Eighteen months since your last check up. Naughty naughty! Should be a more frequent visitor to your dentist.

WOMAN: Can't afford it.

DOCTOR: I know, it's dreadful isn't it? Even a thorough clean…

WOMAN: Next?

DOCTOR: Broken limbs?

WOMAN: None.

DOCTOR: Operations?

WOMAN: None.

DOCTOR: Still got your appendix?

WOMAN: Yes.

DOCTOR: Blood pressure?

WOMAN: Normal. [*aside*] But undoubtedly rising.

DOCTOR: Sleep?

WOMAN: Eight hours. Every night. Without fail.

DOCTOR: Sex?

WOMAN: Female.

DOCTOR: No. I meant have you had sex. In the last 24 hours?

WOMAN: No, look, I'm sorry... I take exception...

DOCTOR: Yes, sorry. It's not for the ID card. Just some private research I'm doing on the side.

WOMAN: Well you can fuck off.

DOCTOR: I'll take that as a no, then. And finally: distinguishing marks.

WOMAN: Marks?

DOCTOR: Tattoos, moles, birthmarks and scars. Self-harm or accidental. So if you wouldn't mind removing all your clothes.

WOMAN: Excuse me! You're not...

DOCTOR: No, no, no. I leave that to the Identity Squad!

The ***Identity Squad*** Sequence.

***LX** change, **music** ["Simmer Down" – jolly Ska], slow-motion, exaggerated movements.*

***Warden** and **Official** appear, long, black coats with plastic gloves that they pull and "snap", dancing to the beat. They grab hold of **Woman** and **Doctor** injects her with a giant syringe. **Woman** becomes floppy and they mime stripping her. They check her for marks and then lift her up for the **Doctor** to inspect – he is now up on the high desk. They bring her **DSC**, help her to stand alone, **Warden** exits and **Official** gives her a card to read. **Doctor** joins them and throws confetti over her. She stands, swaying as **Doctor** and **Official** exit and **LX** changes.*

4.

*The **Woman** is standing in **o/h spot**, picking confetti from her hair. Behind her, and to one side of her, just out of the light, Warden has appeared as **Agent**, dressed in dark suit and dark glasses.*

WOMAN: I am a citizen of the United Kingdom of Great Britain and Northern Ireland. My name is... [*coughs*] My number is 53427349/81. On receiving this Identification Card I accept full citizenship of this country. I agree that those who do not have an Identification Card are second class citizens. I promise to obey the laws of the land particularly those in relation to the prevention of terrorism. I will be vigilant at all times and report to the authorities any second class citizen about whom I have suspicions, however trivial they may seem.

Moving forward slightly she fixes her gaze on someone in the audience.

WOMAN: I will... I... Erm... can I have some more light? Please? More light. [*House **LX** up.*

Pointing] That's him/her. There. Sitting in the third row. I recognize him/her. [*shouting*] He's/she's a terrorist! Arrest him/her!

AGENT: [*moving into audience*] Excuse me sir/madam. Will you come with me, please? Don't make a fuss. The building is surrounded.

***Blackout*.**

Monitor Thirteen

Monitor Thirteen

by   Peter Yates

©COPYRIGHT 2007, 2009 Peter Yates

First Published 2009 by Random Cactus
ISBN: 978-0-9559924-0-7

Rights of Performance are controlled by: Random Cactus
New Place,
Romeland Hill,
St. Albans,
Herts.
AL3 4ET
Phone: 01727 838540
Fax: 01727 843540
Email: random_cactus@yahoo.co.uk
Web: www.randomcactus.co.uk

from whom a license for performance should be obtained.

It is an infringement of the Copyright to give any performance or public reading of the play before the license has been issued.

Characters:

Leach

Hunt

A Shopping Mall Security Monitoring Station.

A shopping mall.

Leach & *Hunt* *are sitting next to each other on chairs **dsc** looking into the audience. They each have a tub of popcorn which they dip into absent-mindedly from time to time. They are watching CCTV monitors. They have ear-pieces and walkie-talkies.*

Light is dim, flickering. The faint sounds of muzak can be heard constantly in the background.

LEACH: Screen three. What's that guy doing?

HUNT: Where?

LEACH: He's round the side of the sweet stall. In that dead corner. Where there isn't a shop.

HUNT: The boarded up bit. Yeah.

LEACH: What's he doing?

HUNT: Er... can't see. Get a close up.

Leach uses remote.

LEACH: He's... he's...

HUNT: He's taking a leak!

LEACH: No.

HUNT: He is, you know. Cheeky bastard. Look you can see...

LEACH: He keeps looking around. Doesn't think anyone can see him.

HUNT: Sorry mate! We can see you! You're pissing in a public shopping mall! You can get arrested for that!

LEACH: Let's get Stone over to him.

HUNT: Where is Stone?

LEACH: Er... screen sixteen. By Smiths.

HUNT: Too far. What about Reed?

LEACH: Can't see him. Anywhere. No.

HUNT: Must be on a break.

LEACH: Perhaps <u>he's</u> taking a leak.

They laugh. **Leach** *writes something on a pad and then secretively writes something in a small notebook.*

HUNT: Hold on...hold on... Screen seven. Kid in hoodie.

Leach *picks up walkie-talkie.*

LEACH: Stone! Stone! Come in Stone! Do you copy? Kid in Hoodie. Outside Karen Millen. Moving quickly towards East Mall. Over.

HUNT: Stone's on the move. Yeah. Should intercept him... just outside.

LEACH: Screen eight...

HUNT: …the Body Shop.

LEACH: Yep. There he goes. Well done, Stone, mate.

HUNT: That's it, Stone, un-hood the little bastard. Close up, Leach.

LEACH: [*using remote*] There. Uh-oh!

HUNT: It's a woman!

LEACH: It's a little old lady. [*listening to w/t*] What's that, Stone? Copy that. [*to **Hunt***] She's very cold.

HUNT: [*sarcastic*] Aaah.

LEACH: Needs to keep her ears and head warm in the snow.

HUNT: What's Stone gonna do? Oi-oi - he's got his scissors out!

LEACH: He's gonna cut it off!

HUNT: Little old lady's protesting...

LEACH: ...small crowd gathering...

HUNT: ...they're all laughing...

LEACH: ...and snip snip snip!

HUNT: Off comes the hood!

LEACH: Nice one Stone!

HUNT: Rules are rules.

LEACH: No hoodies in the mall.

HUNT: Off she goes. A little wiser.

LEACH: And a helluva lot colder.

HUNT: And Stone can add it to his trophy wall.

LEACH: Yeah! [*high fives*] Hey! Crumpet alert!

HUNT: Where?

LEACH: Number two.

HUNT: Oh, man! Just take a look at that. She must be a model or something.

LEACH: Blonde, tall, long legs, mini-skirt and particularly well endowed.

HUNT: What?

LEACH: Well stacked.

HUNT: Yeah. Do you think they're real?

LEACH: Oh, yeah. Definitely.

HUNT: Tenner says they're not.

LEACH: Yeah?

HUNT: Yeah.

LEACH: You're on. [*shake*] Let's find out.

HUNT: Look, Reed's back on the scene – he's right near her.

LEACH: Knowing Reed he's been following her throughout the mall.

HUNT: [*into w/t*] Come in Reed. Reed? Do you copy? Leggy blonde. She's been shoplifting.

Leach *laughs.*

LEACH: Here he goes.

HUNT: Takes her into the back of the shop.

LEACH: Camera twenty-one.

HUNT: Right. Puts down bag.

LEACH: Reed goes through it.

HUNT: Coat comes off.

LEACH: Top comes off. Good, good.

HUNT: Ah, what's he saying.

LEACH: He's shaking his head at the camera.

HUNT: Shit. We're fucked.

LEACH: [*into w/t*] Reed! All the way, please. We have a bet on here.

HUNT: Here he goes.

LEACH: Off it comes.

HUNT: He's very thorough.

LEACH: Ok, here we go…

HUNT: …come on…a bit more…

LEACH: …further,

HUNT/LEACH: …further… and… Yes!

HUNT: Oh, man!

LEACH: Score! And... I think that's a tenner you owe me.

Hunt hands over tenner.

HUNT: OK. But It was worth every penny!

LEACH: Thanks Reed. Pint waiting for you. Over. Hey up! What's he doing? He's getting her number! The conniving bastard.

HUNT: Leach...

LEACH: How many times does he do that...?

HUNT: Leach...

LEACH: It must be the sympathetic way he treats them.

HUNT: Leach...

LEACH: "I'm really sorry to have to do this madam. There's probably been some mistake..."

HUNT: Leach!

LEACH: What?

HUNT: Monitor 13. There's a bloke. He looks... exactly like you.

LEACH: What?

HUNT: Look. [*using remote*] Close up. Sitting there. On a chair. Next to...

LEACH: Hey, you're right. He does look like me. And the bloke he's sitting next to...

HUNT: Fuck.

LEACH: Looks exactly like you.

HUNT: Look. This is some kind of wind-up...

LEACH: We're... naked...

HUNT: And we're... tied to the chairs. Our hands..

LEACH: …and legs are chained.

HUNT: You're bleeding. Badly. From the head.

LEACH: And you've got horrible marks, wounds all over your body.

HUNT: I don't like this, Leach.

LEACH: If this is some elaborate hoax…

HUNT: Fuck! What was that?

LEACH: That guy, big burly guy, he's hitting us with a stick or…

HUNT: It's a fucking truncheon!

LEACH: Steady on mate! You're gonna break… he is breaking our fingers!

HUNT: He looks like…

LEACH: It's Stone!

HUNT: Call him! Call him up.

LEACH: [into w/t] Stone? Stone? Come in Stone. Do you copy?

HUNT: Look – he's picking up his walkie-talkie. He's speaking. What's he saying?

LEACH: "Shut the fuck up. You're next. Over".

HUNT: Hey - this other guy – he's got a syringe.

LEACH: He's going to… he's going to inject us.

HUNT: We're struggling. We don't want to be injected.

LEACH: Oh, fuck. Don't do it to me, please.

HUNT: Please no. Sweet Jesus. Don't inject me.

LEACH: I'll tell you everything.

HUNT: Everything you want to know.

LEACH: I must be dreaming. This is a horrible nightmare.

HUNT: But I'm having it too. We can't be having simultaneous nightmares.

LEACH: It's real. It's too real.

HUNT: Ahh! No! No! He's going to inject me! The bastard! Ahh!

LEACH: It's Reed! He's punched you in the mouth. Syringe at the ready. And now Stone's going to inject me! No! Please! [*into w/t*] Look, Stone, Reed, please. It wasn't me. Honestly. It wasn't me. It's Hunt. He's the one. He fabricates the evidence. Doctors the videos. Doesn't report the young girl shoplifters if they'll have sex with him. Not me. I just...

HUNT: [*fighting for w/t*] You lying bastard, Leach. You fucking, snivelling grass! You're in it up to your neck. Who sells the tapes on the black market? Who blackmails the perps with the videos? You've already got that guy who took a leak in your little black book! Who's got an illegal deal with a satellite channel for the Shopping Mall Reality TV show?

LEACH/HUNT: Ahh! He's injecting me!

HUNT: [*looks at **Leach***] Bastard.

LEACH: [*looks at **Hunt***] Bastard.

The door opens. They turn and stare, clinging onto each other in fear as the shaft of light from the door illuminates them.

Blackout.

Other Plays by Peter Yates:

Gullibility Factor
Crazy Patterns
The Reality Checker
Urban Cycles [trilogy: *Dignity*, *Wages Day*, *Real Gone Kid*. Co-writer Jenny Wafer]
Big Yellow Taxi

www.randomcactus.co.uk

www.ingramcontent.com/pod-product-compliance
Ingram Content Group UK Ltd.
Pitfield, Milton Keynes, MK11 3LW, UK
UKHW041435180426
11947UKWH00007B/453